Rumi & Lily: An Internet Love Story

by Rumi Noir & Lily Schott Sweetdog

To Anella

Rumi & Lily: An Internet Love Story

(Not for children)

from the late great Rumi Noir

by Rumi Noir & Lily Schott Sweetdog

and your grateful friend Jean with love.

typed by Penelope Scambly Schott & Jean Anaporte

illustrated by Sophie Franz

Jean Anaporte

12 May 2013

Rumi & Lily: An Internet Love Story

copyright 2012 by Penelope Scambly Schott & Jean Anaporte
All rights reserved

ISBN paperback: 978-1-937493-24-0
ISBN eBook: 978-1937493-33-2
Library of Congress Control Number: 2012945038

Schott, Penelope Scambly, and Anaporte, Jean
Rumi & Lily: An Internet Love Story
1. Title; 2. Dogs-Fiction; 3. Dog correspondence-email; 4.Companion animals-fiction; 5. Gender relations-fiction; 6. Animal humor; 7. Dog romance; 8. Dying

Cover art and interior book illustrations by Sophie Franz
Cover production by Jana Westhusing/StudioBlue West
Book design by Carla Perry
Printed in the United States of America

DANCING MOON PRESS
P.O. Box 832
Newport, OR 97365
541-574-7708
info@dancingmoonpress.com / www.dancingmoonpress.com

First Edition

DEDICATION

To Rumi Noir, and Penelope's mother, and Rumi's beloved Lily.

SOME OTHER WRITINGS BY TYPISTS PENELOPE SCAMBLY SCHOTT & JEAN ANAPORTE

Penelope Scambly Schott

Novel: *A Little Ignorance*

Chapbooks: *My Grandparents Were Married for Sixty-Five Years, These Are My Same Hands, Wave Amplitude in the Mona Passage, Almost Learning to Live in this World, Under Taos Mountain*

Full-length poetry collections: *The Perfect Mother, Baiting the Void, May the Generations Die in the Right Order, Six Lips, Crow Mercies*

Narratives in verse: *Penelope: The Story of the Half-Scalped Women, The Pest Maiden: A Story of Lobotomy, A is for Anne: Mistress Hutchinson Disturbs the Commonwealth*

Jean Anaporte

Poetry in anthologies: *Anthology of Magazine Verse and Yearbook of American Poetry, IndiAnnual, Ithaca Women's Anthology, Letters to the World, Poets Against the War, Wild Sweet Notes: Fifty Years of West Virginia Poetry 1950-1999, With a Fly's Eye, Whale's Wit, & Woman's Heart*

Poetry in journals: *Anima, Arts Indiana, Arts Indiana Literary Supplement, Corrobee, The Flying Island, Glens Falls Review, The Greenfield Review, Groundswell, Kestrel, Kritya, Mildred, One Trick Pony, Poetry in our Time, Poiesie, Thanal, The Refined Savage, 13th Moon, Yellow Silk, Washout Review*

Essays in reference books and journals: *Arts Indiana, Callaloo, Contemporary Literary Criticism 2002, Groundswell, Mid-American Review, Poetry Criticism, XVII, 13th Moon, Written Communication,* and forthcoming book: *Breathing from the Belly: Etheridge Knight on Poetry and Freedom*

INTRODUCTION

This is a completely true internet love story, except dogs don't type.

Once upon a time, some women on the Internet were discussing gender differences. Jean wrote, *Women apologize too much. I even apologize to my dog.*

Someone else on the list asked, *What did you do to your dog?*

Penelope wrote, *She probably stepped on him. Because dogs want to be exactly where you are.* And she signed it—*Penelope (owned by Lily)*, because dog-people are owned by their dogs.

Jean posted a response. *Hey, he's a guy. I'm the one who wants to be closer to him.*

And then A WONDERFUL THING happened! Jean's dog, Rumi, sent an email to Penelope's dog, Lily. Read on to see what came next....

Mon, Mar 30, 2009 10:26 pm
To: Lily Schott Sweetdog
From: Rumi Noir
Subject: human females

Dear Lily,

What do you think? Do you, as a bitch, like your human female more than you like me, a *macho*? Actually I like mine a lot. She's my second. It was the human male stuck to my first female that I couldn't stand. He got jealous because I sat between them on the couch.

Some human males piss me off if they don't salute me. Most females quiver and go *ooo* and *aahhhhhh* and stoop to stroke me because they think I'm the most beautiful dog in the world. I realize nobody thinks that of you. I'm the most beautiful. You might be the second most. I'm a standard poodle, but I don't swim. I caught a mallard by the neck once. He flapped his wings in my face, the bastard. Anyway, he got away.

I'm in West Virginia—wherever that is. Where are you? I'm 45 pounds and *fixed*—whatever that means. I am very sexy. Did you say where you are?
Woof-Boof, Rumi Noir

Even though it was much too late at night, Lily responded within minutes.

Mon, Mar 30, 2009 10:40 PM
To: Rumi Noir
From: Lily Schott Sweetdog
Subject: Re: human females

Dear Rumi N.

Thank you for your letter. This is just a quick lick and promise that I'll write to you in the morning. My people are about to go to bed and if I don't get there first, I don't get the spot in between them. It's all a bit tricky because we have a double bed and I weigh 52 pounds.

Oh, and you may be the most beautiful dog in West Virginia, but I am the most beautiful dog in Oregon. (We shall politely ignore the foolish human who said I look like a Dr. Seuss dog.)

Happy dreams.

Your new pen pal,
Lily

Tue, Mar 31, 2009 10:16 AM
To: Rumi Noir
From: Lily Schott Sweetdog
Subject: Re: human females

Hey, Rumi,

Don't pull that macho stuff with me—a mallard, big deal. I dug up a mole yesterday. It wiggled its pink hands for a long time before it stopped. My people didn't even say anything about the hole in the front yard. Of course, we don't have grass, just stones. In fact, I sometimes rearrange the stones into fancy patterns. Then the people are very impressed and call it *Doghenge.* So far, I haven't been able to find out what that means.

What's *sexy*? I don't know anything about sex. Unless you mean that bouncy stuff they do on the bed. It wakes me up but I pretend not to look. Smells pretty interesting. But this is getting awfully personal. Let's get to an issue of national importance: Who will be chosen First Dog?

I am happy to have a pen pal in West Virginia, wherever that is. I'm in the upper left hand corner.

Love, Lily
p.s. Please don't take offense at the macho comment. I hope you can take a joke.

If we are going to be friends, we need to trust each other. If I had a real complaint about you, I'd say it clearly and politely. Just setting the ground rules.

Wed, Apr 1, 2009 8:52 PM
To: Lily Schott Sweetdog
From: Rumi Noir
Subject: Re: human females

Wow—Lily,

It's been a while since I got a quick lick. Jean says I scare female and male dogs. But not you. Boof-Woof!!!!

There's a place called Oregon and you're the most beautiful dog there?!

Wow! I thought I was the most beautiful dog in the World. Jean says maybe not because some people have lived only in West Virginia.

Well, I'll sleep on it. Knowing there are parallel universes is a blow.

Hmmm. Can a macho guy dog give quick licks? This is really new.

Rumi Noir
p.s. I'm glad you do email. RN

Thu, Apr 2, 2009, 7:28 pm
To: Lily Schott Sweetdog
From: Rumi Noir
Subject: Re: human females

<It wiggled its pink hands for a long time before it stopped.>
Wow! Jean would have made me open my mouth if the animal wiggled its fingers. One time she was walking a dog that grabbed and bit down on a baby groundhog till it stopped wiggling its toes, and she cried out loud the whole walk while the dog (a curly-back Chow) pranced proudly the whole time, pulling her to walk faster.

But I am macho. I even had a poem published.

Big Poodle Rock Star
I can growl better than Randy Newman,
hit higher notes than the Bee Gees,
bite words sharper than Bob Dylan. When I
lift my leg—forget Mick Jagger. My furred
prepuce fits snugger than Jim Morrison's
leather pants, and when I feel the fire,
my coral tip slips out.
　　　　　　　　　　—by Rumi Noir, Poet

See what I mean? It also shows that I know about sex. I get put out of our bedroom when Jean has sex. I jumped on the man the first time I saw Jean kiss him. He said I looked like a black torpedo coming over her shoulder. I think about that when I'm in my crate.

If you arrange stones, you must be an artist. That's better than being the dog that bit the groundhog to death. And you're either pink or white because you're Lily. I've never met a pink dog and I'm a poodle. What are you? A Dr. Seuss?

Sniffs and Licks (I wish I really could),
Rumi Noir

8

Thu, Apr 2, 2009 11:23 PM
To: Rumi Noir
From: Lily Schott Sweetdog
Subject: Re: human females

Oh, Rumi,

I can tell you are one hot poodle. But I'll let you in on a secret—my people can rub my belly really well because I don't have one of those stupid penises in the way.

Although our relationship is likely to remain intellectual, I suppose it doesn't hurt to tell you I am white (well, sort of white—in the snow I look champagne-colored) and have a magnificent plume of a tail.

Penelope says I have to get off the computer now because she has to catch a plane early tomorrow morning to go visit her mother. She promises she'll be home on Tuesday and that I can get back on the computer after that. Meanwhile, feel free to write to me.

Goodnight.

What do you smell like?

Love, Lily

Fri, Apr 03, 2009 10:25 pm
To: Lily Schott Sweetdog
From: Rumi Noir
Re: human females

Dear Lily,

<What do you smell like?>

Now, that's personal.

The only things that Jean smells are my feet (*Fritos*), my body (*a sweater*—I'm a poodle, remember), my mouth *(not unbearable/foul)*—some of these words I don't understand—and my ears *(need medicine/don't need medicine)*. She's uptight, so she's never really smelled me where she'd learn anything. That's why humans stay dumb—well, out of it.

Champagne on snow—Brrrr Woof-Boof. Jean showed me where you live. Too far to trot, she said. And an ocean. I never learned to swim, but I did scratch Jean all over her chest and arms when she tried to teach me. I prefer running in the water and shouting at the ducks, and making long leaps back to shore when I can't look at them b/c I have to hold my nose above water.

So, what about you? What do you smell like, I mean. Oh, Lily!

Rumi Noir

Sun, Apr 05, 2009 12:45 am
To: Lily Schott Sweetdog
From: Rumi Noir
Subject: stupid penises

Dear Lily,

How can you know penises are stupid if you don't have one (or have never shared one)? Have you?

I know my penis is smart. Everything that excites me excites him—female dogs, female humans, guy humans, guy dogs (sometimes), cars, being chased by my human—I can't remember the rest.

Listen, Lily, I don't know about *intellectual*. A plume-like tail, eh? (I'm panting and other things are happening. My tongue is much wider and longer. *Et cetera*. (I know a little Latin.)

Yours, Rumi Noir

Tue, Apr 07, 2009 12:12 pm
To: Rumi Noir
From: Lily Schott Sweetdog
Subject: Dear Rumi

Dear Rumi Noir,

I am using your whole name because it sounds so distinguished. Or should I say—since I too am a multi-lingual dog—so *distingué.*

Have you ever thought about the expression *multi-lingual?* If they were dog tongues, imagine how much lovely pink dog tongue that could be. And yes, I know, yours is wide and long. All the guys say that.

But I should let up on the male-bashing. I suppose having one center of sensation simplifies your life. Meanwhile, I keep hoping good things will happen to my belly, under my chin, and oh, my ears.

Often I have to plonk down on top of my people to remind them. In the middle of the night, I flop my head from her leg to his leg, and since my head is full of heavy thoughts, they sometimes wake up a little and rub me. Does that work with your people?

Going back to the discussion of smell, I do the best I can to feel and smell attractive. Whenever I find a dead animal, I roll on it. The beach generally provides a dead seagull or two. The only smell I truly dislike is soap. About three times a year they send me to a torture chamber where a mean lady attacks me with a hose and soap and sprayer and then she gets out a pair of clippers and steals my curls. I bet she sells them.

Okay, my person is bugging me to get off the computer because she got home from her mother's house late last night and claims she has 275 new email messages.

Love, Lily
p.s. My whole name is
    Lily Schott Sweetdog.

Apr 09, 2009 1:10 AM
To: Lily Schott Sweetdog
From: Rumi Noir
Subject: Re: Dear Rumi

Dear Lily S. Sweetdog,

Hang on, I'm coming, I'm coming.

I am not *distingué*; I am **macho**. (Yes, that print was supposed to be big.) My tongue is very pink, very long, very skinny. My human says it's like an aardvark tongue. Very sexy!

I think you have a more liberal human than I do. I never get to roll in shit or dead fish or anything else b/c she's afraid I'll jump off the dead fish and run like fire after a car. Or truck. Trucks turn me on, baby. I'm a Standard Poodle and the Goddesses know it—I can do these things. She disagrees rudely. In February, I got loose from a tree while she was shoveling snow and I attacked a car. I admit I was a little fuzzy in the head afterwards. A neighbor drove us to the vet while my human cooed in the back seat with me. Really! She's besotted.

She says I survived only b/c the snow was too deep for the car to go fast. She doesn't understand my power. I love her, but she's uptight. You know what I mean? You don't always have to smell them to know. And that's another thing—how she pushes me away when she's bare.

I forgive you for being jealous. I have a very sexy penis and I would share it with you if I could get to you. Do you have a map?

Heavy thoughts. . . . My head is full of flashing teeth. I'm a guy.

Thu, Apr 09, 2009 4:59 PM
To: Rumi Noir
From: Lily Schott Sweetdog
Subject: Dear Rumi

Dear Rumi,

Again, your persistent emphasis on machismo. Do you have any idea what you are talking about? I went to the dictionary (it's hard with paws, as you know—I had to use my tongue to turn pages), and here's what it says about Macho:

Adjective
1. *having or characterized by qualities considered Manly, esp. when manifested in an assertive, self-conscious, or dominating way*
2. *having a strong or exaggerated sense of power or the right to dominate*

Noun
3. *assertive or aggressive manliness; machismo*

Manly is fine (I, for example, am very womanly), but *dominating* and *exaggerated sense of power* aren't so good. You might want to reconsider.

Before I go further, let me announce that I don't want this letter to be about penises. It makes me feel left out.

Going back to tongues, I have never seen an aardvark or its tongue. I have, however, seen a frog's tongue. Wahoo, can it move fast!

As for maps, just look up the Lewis and Clark expedition. They came pretty close to my house. Most important, Captain Merry Weather Lewis came with his dog Seaman. Although history books omit this important fact, Seaman was in charge of the whole expedition.

More soon.
Love, Lily

Thu, Apr 9, 2009 8:20 PM
To: Lily Schott Sweetdog
From: Rumi Noir
Subject: Dear Rumi

Ms. Sweetdog—

You wrote: *<Before I go any further, let me announce that I don't want this letter to be about penises.>*
I counted. You have talked about penises in three letters. I've mentioned them in two. I did write *coral tip* in my poem, but you started a whole other letter under the title, *Stupid Penises.* That's mean. My human said maybe you called them stupid b/c you are jealous. She said Freud is not always wrong. She said Freud was a man with a cigar in place of a penis—or something like that. So, all right already. If you don't want your letters to be about penises, stop insulting them and stop bringing them up. Then they won't be in our letters.

Mr. Noir

Thu, Apr 09, 2009 11:08 PM
To: Lily Schott Sweetdog
From: Rumi Noir
Subject: Dear Rumi

Dear Lily S. Sweetdog:

Lemme explain. My human may be a feminist, but I am a guy dog. A dictionary is a book. I don't care what's in books unless they taste good or give lots of chewing pleasure. My human is grateful that I leave her books alone; I am grateful that she doesn't want me to look at the words.

Multi-lingual: I've never thought about that expression. I find myself more interested in *many-tongued*. Think what you could do with more than one!

You didn't even say you were sorry I lost in the crash with the car. I mean, I've got a heart. It was 1955 pounds against 45 pounds. Is *underdog* in your dictionary?

R. Noir

Fri, Apr 10, 2009 8:44 AM
Subject: Re: Dear Rumi

Dear Underdog,

I was discreetly ignoring your indiscretion with the aforesaid vehicle.
'Nuf said.

Respectfully, Ms. L.S. Sweetdog, PhD[*]

p.s. Okay, I was trying to be a hard-nose, but really I am a wet-nose, and I
have begun to care about you enough that I am relieved you were not
seriously injured in that unfortunate encounter.

---

[*] PhD = Pretty happy Dog!

Fri, Apr 10, 2009 9:39 AM
To: Rumi Noir
From: Lily Schott Sweetdog
Subject: addendum

Dear Rumi,

I just got back from my morning constitutional. Clearing my bowels tends to clear my brain as well.

(BTW, do you have the same problem I do in deciding where to leave the morning offering? I tend to sniff around a bit, and turn a circle before finding the right spot. When my person squats in the woods, she's not so fussy. Mainly she goes behind a tree.)

Anyhow, all of this is leading up to an addendum to my last message. Perhaps my tone was a bit high and mighty. I should admit that I, too, occasionally cannot suppress my impulse to chase a car. I try to be ladylike, but I have also been known to flatulate. (In case your vocabulary is not as extensive as mine, I mean fart.) Okay, that's my confession for the day. Time for my nap.

Love, Lily

Fri, Apr 10, 2009 11:43 AM
To: Lily Schott Sweetdog
From: Rumi Noir
Subject: Re: addendum

Dear Champagne-on-Snow Lily,

I was so happy to get two letters from you that were not only gentle, but about me. Really. And so many interesting things to talk about, too.

I enjoy looking for the right place to clear my bowels—how delicately you put it. For me it's finding the place with the best smells so I can relax and really enjoy the release. My human wants a tree with lots of leafy things around, but nothing underneath her (she's afraid of all varieties of ivy). She takes a long time finding the right spot, and sometimes tells me I am a lucky dog. (You know, the p. thing.)

If you occasionally chase cars, you might understand my compulsion to prove that I am not afraid and am in fact fiercer than they are—especially trucks. *Rowwwoooo.* They inflame me.

Licks and love, Rumi

Fri, Apr 10, 2009 12:57 PM
To: Rumi Noir
From: Lily Schott Sweetdog
Subject: Re: addendum

Dear Rumi,

    Champagne-on-Snow. IMHO, you really *are* a poet. Maybe I'm falling in love. Be careful of those trucks—I wouldn't want to lose you.

Long slow licks and excited little quick ones, Lily

Fri, Apr 10, 2009
To: Lily Schott Sweetdog
From: Rumi Noir
Subject: Re: addendum

Ohhhh, Lily,

You've melted me. You can even say *stupid penis* once in a while.

(sniffs and licks) Rumi

Wed, Apr 15, 2009 11:06 AM
To: Rumi Noir
From: Lily Schott Sweetdog
Subject: The Morning After

Dear Rumi Noir,

I don't know what to say. Here I went and opened my heart to you, and what do I get? Silence. Five long, heart-breaking days of silence.

Did you just enjoy the chase? I'm not a car to be chased just for the fun of it. I have heard about males who pursue young women and then disappear. I don't want to think that of you.

I know I said ours was an intellectual friendship, but I still feel rejected. Is it because I don't like poetry? I asked you to reconsider your macho values. Maybe I could reconsider poetry.

Okay, I've already made enough of a fool of myself. I won't beg. But I'll sit.

Your erstwhile friend, Lily

Wed, Apr 15, 2009 8:47 PM
To: Lily Schott Sweetdog
From: Rumi Noir
Subject: Re: The Morning After

Lily!

I signed on just to write to you! I haven't been able to get to the email machine! She's been pigging it (I know, that's species-ist).

Here's how it is:

Sunday was all Sun. We walked by the river. Out of a million smells, I know the names for only the two she knows—green for daffodils; delirious sweet for honeysuckle. (They had lots of other smells around their roots, but I don't know their names b/c she can't smell them.)

And then at the river, we saw two duck couples. I barked my heart and pride out. I could have nabbed them but she wouldn't let me free. And they were **male** and **female**. Twice. And I thought of you up in the left-hand corner, and it hurt the heart in my stern-shaped chest. I couldn't catch them and I couldn't have you.

So Monday and Tuesday and Wednesday it rained, and that's how it felt in my chest, so I was rolling around on my back on her bed making *arrrrawh* noises when I fell off and hurt my leg. She lifted me back on, but I was humiliated. Humiliated! I'm glad you weren't there.

Then a little boy on our sidewalk looked at me and said, *He's bumpy!* His grandmother (quite a dish for a human) said, *Yes, he has curly hair.* Oh, Lily, I need you.

On a calmer note, there's a dogwood tree in our yard, as is the case in a lot of yards on this sidewalk (we don't have a road & Jean is glad). For two springs, I've tried to understand this—the tree is wood, so the white and pink things at the top must be dogs? They don't smell like dogs, they don't look like dogs. They are pink and white. Is that what you look like? How do you get down to roll in shit?

Oh, Lily, you misunderstand me. Can you fly here next weekend? East End, sidewalk, Jean's house (and mine), Charleston.

Lily, I love you.
Rumi Noir

Sat, Apr 18, 2009 8:54 AM
To: Rumi Noir
From: Lily Schott Sweetdog
Subject: Re: the Morning After

Dear Rumi,

Just a thought—if your person put her nose closer to the ground, she would know more. I always put my nose under the leaves. Then, if there's a good smell, I know where to roll. I've had some lovely green goop on my shoulder for two days. Fortunately, it doesn't come off with soap.

I know exactly where your heart is because I have a chest like a boat keel with my heart toward the leeward side. (I like to sound nautical. It's jaunty.)

Male and female ducks, eh? The males are prettier, I think. Why do you suppose creatures come in two kinds? As far as I can tell, being female mainly saves me from having to pee so often. I squat. Do you?

My person says we can't come see you now but maybe sometime. She says you and I are pen pals. She says she has to go to her mother in New York again this week. She says a lot of words, actually. I pretend to listen. I listen better when she has a cookie for me.

But today, I listened without getting a cookie. She had big, wet eyes like me. She says her mother is dying. I didn't know what to do, so I licked her nose and it was salty. I suppose I once had a mother but I don't remember her. When I was a pup, I thought the sheepskin on the back of the couch was my mother.

I better make my person go eat breakfast. You and I have important jobs. I'm so glad we are still friends. Any kind of licks you like best, maybe some sticky, stinky ones,

Lily

p.s. If I could, I'd share the green goop with you.

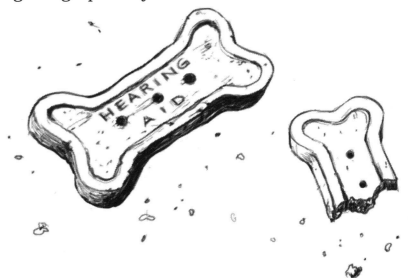

Sat, Apr 18, 2009 11:38 PM
To: Lily Schott Sweetdog
From: Rumi Noir
Subject: Re: the Morning After

Lily,

Thank you for offering to share the green goop. If I lived by you, I'd joyously have green goop, too.

I know what you mean—I pretend to listen. Actually, I have my brain programmed for certain words like *treat, walk, breakfast,* and so on.

I also know about those big wet human eyes. I was one year old when my first human, Mommy Ann, had a bad thing happen. A car killed her baby (big, you know, like them).

Hey! I just had a BIG thought—maybe that's the reason why I want to get cars and trucks so much.

So then Mommy Ann's eyes were squinty and wet and I think I did things wrong. I kept inviting her to play. I think that's why I'm with Jean now.

I don't remember my mother. At first, I lived with someone named CJ, who was blind, and whom I thought was my father. He died but I was still alive. I liked to copy him, but he couldn't see.

I think a dying mother is like a human leaving us so that we never live with them again. I thought I would die when my Mommy Ann left me with a white-haired human I'd seen once, who kept wanting to hold me while I leapt and spun all over the room. After they gave me to her, I was nice for a while, then I went crazy for a long time.

I think that's what having a mother die is like. You are very wise to lick tears, Lily. Humans think licking is loving. Maybe it is. I'm not very into love stuff. I'd had enough when she drove off, and the way she treated me when her male was around... *GRRRRRRRR*. I still have trouble with those two. If a mother is dying, that means she's leaving where she lives and everywhere she could live, right? I'd like to write you that she isn't dying. I still get to see my Mommy Ann. In this case, it isn't your human, but your human's mother who is dying. That's very scary.

I don't know what to say. You have a big, important job. I'm glad you know where my heart is, and I'm glad yours is there, too. My human has hers on the leeward side like us. I don't know if they all do. She's too huggy for me. I'm a Poodle male. I prefer girl dogs.

I'm sad for what's happening to you and your woman. If your woman is sad, it'll make you sad. My human was sick and went away twice in the cold time. She didn't even tell me that she was going. Her friend came and patted me. It seemed like a long, long, long, long time that day before she came back.

But dying means *No, you leave and stay where you went. You never come back.* I don't like to be hugged, but I want to stay with my human.

I send you whatever licks you need, plus tail swishes, and play-bows, and paw pats. We are not pen pals. We are male and female dogs. That is, we are magnets that fly together.

I am your man.
Love, Rumi Noir

Sun, Apr 19, 2009 2:27 PM
To: Lily Schott Sweetdog
From: Rumi Noir
Subject: Re: The Morning After

<Male and female ducks. The males are prettier, I think.>

Dear Lily,

Of course they are. And Jean gets so mad because she likes the way females look better, but everyone who walks by us says how beautiful I am. She gets disgusted. It's hard sticking up for females, isn't it?

Unless you're a guy, of course. Guy Dogs like me love female dogs *and* female humans.

Do you still have green goop? I wish I could sniff (& shyly lick) it, Lily.

Love,
Rumi Noir, The Guy Dog

Sun, Apr 26, 2009 9:08 PM
To: Rumi Noir
From: Lily Schott Sweetdog
Subject: Re: The Morning After

Dear Rumi,

It's different with ducks. Their equipment is hidden, so they have to show the male-female difference on the outside. I'm sure your equipment isn't hidden.

Actually, I'd rather talk about ducks and sex, but I have to tell you something else—my person says her mother has died. I don't know exactly what *died* is, but it doesn't sound good.

Anyhow, she says that's why she hasn't turned the computer on for me in so many days. She went to see her mother and came home with her hands all scratched and bleached from cleaning her mother's house. She's tired now. I will make sure to lie close to her tonight and lick her face if she needs it. Sometimes she cries and sometimes she laughs, but it's not like regular laughing.

Like I said before, you and I have a big job, Rumi. It's hard work taking care of our people.

Even though I have a good excuse, I'll try not to be so delinquent in my correspondence.
Goodnight.

Love, Lily

p.s. Dogwood is a lie. It has nothing to do with dogs. We don't even pee near it more often than we pee on other trees.

p.p.s. What kind of collar do you wear? Mine is pink with darker pink polka dots. At first, I was embarrassed to wear it, but it does give me a coquettish air.

Sun, Apr 26, 2009 10:05 PM
To: Lily Schott Sweetdog
From: Rumi Noir
Subject: Re: The Morning After

Dear Lily Dog Flower,

My human told me why she thought you weren't writing to me. So this human of yours is lucky. You do have a big job, but you sound wise and intelligent.

I'm a guy. I sometimes get bored with my human's feelings. But I pull it together when I think it's serious.

I'm glad your human is back to turn on the computer. I don't know what to say about death. The daughter in my first house went away in a car and never came back and my woman (she is Mommy Anne) went to bed for months. Did I tell you all this already?

There was a black and grey standard poodle in that house who couldn't see but who taught me where to smell things and when to listen to the humans. Then he went away and never came back. No one explained it, but Jean says the poodle died.

<Mine is pink with darker pink polka dots. At first I was embarrassed to

wear it, but it does give me a coquettish air.>

Wow! Boof-Woof!! I know you have that air even though I've never smelled you. That's why I refuse to be a pen pal. And those ducks know how to smell, don't they?

I have a collar with cows on it which looks good against my black fur, and a purple collar that women say is sexy. They are called *cow collar* and *purple collar.* I don't wear either one at night. I have to come and hold still in the morning while she puts one on. The other is usually being washed (I stick my head in lots of holes).

I'm very interested to hear that dogwood is fake dog. Why didn't Jean tell me?

Oh! You're right. My equipment isn't hidden, and I slide it out sometimes to make sure it's working right. It always is.

Many sniffs and licks,
Rumi Noir

Sat, May 23, 2009 1:48 PM
To: Rumi Noir
From: Lily Schott Sweetdog
Subject: Dear Rumi

Dear Rumi,

You should have been here yesterday. I had a great day. Both doors were wide open all day and five furnace men walked in and out with big square things and long pointy things and they all said hello to me and some of them patted me several times even though I barked every time they walked by. (I knew it was the same people over and over, but I was demonstrating that I was on duty.) I got to lie on the sticky parts of the fallen rhododendron blossoms and was covered with these brown pod things (which show up effectively on my white curls, if you don't mind my saying so), and every time I came back in I sprinkled them all over the floor and rugs. Like I said, a great day.

My humans are back from what they call a *memorial,* and they seem real happy to be with me. I lick them a lot and they say they love me. I wonder if I'm starting to love you. I would lick you, too.

Your friend, Lily

Sun, May 24, 2009 12:07 AM
To: Lily Schott Sweetdog
From: Rumi Noir
Subject: Re: Dear Rumi

Dear Lily-Champagne-on-Snow,

Brown pod things in Champagne-on-Snow fur. How cool is that! Then all those people come in and you bark every time, and they bow down, besotted, to pet you. Ah, you. You and me.

And your humans loving you.... This death stuff is getting to me.

My humans love me too. My first human, Mommy Anne, came to see me and I had to jump up to the couch to see her and down from the couch to see Jean. They talked about me, about how when I slept on Cara's bed I fell off a lot b/c I lie on my back. I have a skinny back. Finally, with Jean I learned to prop myself against her when I lie upside down. (I'm very lean and svelte, you see. Well, I guess you can't see, but I wish you could.)

Anyway, I have something difficult to say to you, especially difficult since you just dealt with a death—I have Cancer. My human took me to the doctor and they said everything's fine but two days later she got mad and said, *Everything's not fine,* and back we went to the doctor and he stuck a needle in me. The next week she got a phone call and started dripping tears from her eyes with her mouth open, which makes interesting smells and embarrassing sounds. She hugged me till I could hardly breathe and chanted over and over, *I love you, Rumi.* She loves me. I am brave, I am smart, I am handsome.

Lily, Are you listening? This is important.

I am funny, I am a disgusting alpha male chauvinist pig, and she loves me. Out of her mind. I have the Cancer they think is *fast.* I'm faster, of course, but when I say this she bursts into howls and waters from the eyes, and there's a word for that but I can't remember it. I'm going to die sooner than she wants me to. I sleep a lot. I eat grass—So?! My poops—never mind. I'm tired. I'm a little depressed, except—*Lily, are you listening*—when I think of you. *Champagne-on-Snow with a plumey tail.*

It is fast. They cut a little piece out of me and I didn't say they could. I wore a handsome bright yellow thing for a whole day, and humans and dogs came to me and sniffed and petted. Jean still gets wet around the eyes and makes terrible howling sounds. Lily, I'm telling you: There is no justice. They complain about our barks all the time! But she did boil a cow femur for me today. And gave me four more biscuits than usual, not to mention my second Frosty Paw in a week.

My human lies on the floor and pets me, and didn't get mad at me when a man/boy (I couldn't tell which) came in and put his paw in her purse while she was running her hand down my whole self, I didn't even bark. She does, though. Loud and scary. He dropped the *wallet* and ran. Jean hugged me, and said something into the phone. A nice man who likes poodles came over.

They walked up and down the stairs and looked in closets. When he left, we went for a walk, but not as fast or for as long as we used to.

I'm in charge. It's a trip.

But my body isn't working right—I can't pull her down—and I'm thinking I might never see you, but *Lily, I am one hot alpha handsome poodle male for you.*

More later.

Licks and sniffs,
Rumi Noir

Rumi, Rumi, Rumi, you are making my person drip water out of her eyes. We don't care if you are a male chauvinist dog. We love you. I don't want anything bad to happen to you. (Well, falling off the bed isn't so bad. But here's a hint: when you lie on your back, spread out all your legs for balance—and easier access to belly rubs.) It's scary when humans howl. I try to make them feel better when they do, but it doesn't always work.

This letter is supposed to be about you, but I need advice. I have a problem that happens in the summer and it is starting to happen again. What should I do? Our house has sliding screen doors and I can't tell when they're open or closed. Once I walked into the screen and it went *SPROING* and I got scared. My people laughed at me. Now I stand outside the door and won't go through because I don't know whether the screen is open or shut. Yesterday, my Penelope person got up off the lounge chair and walked through the doorway to show me it was safe.

Here's my question—if the door is open when she goes through, will it be open when I go through? This may sound trivial, but I really do like to go out and in and I don't like being *sproinged* or laughed at. Next time I'll tell you about my problem with the handles on pans.

I guess I'm just trying to change the subject. Really, I don't want you to be sick.

Love, Lily
p.s. I bet you looked great in your yellow thing. You would look great in anything.

Sun, May 24, 2009 6:52 pm
To: Lily Schott Sweetdog
From: Rumi Noir
Subject: Dear Rumi

Dear Lily,

It's true—I look great in my bright yellow thing. I am a very handsome dog even with part of me shaved.

Now, this thing about sliding doors. When we had one, there was a screen. So if the glass was open, I could see the screen and not be embarrassed. It's one of the most horrible things humans do—laugh at us b/c we are so loyal and patient with all their stupid mistakes, like not knowing where a smell comes from or what it is. Or not even knowing there *is* a smell right in their own garden. Jean's always asking me when I walk with my nose close to the grass or dirt, *What are you smelling?* Why does she ask? She knows I won't answer.

They're weird, Lily, and they can be very rude b/c sometimes they're not as smart as they think they are. But they love us—or, at least, the ones I've met love me. And I can tell that your Penelope person loves you b/c she told you about her mother, which is a hard, sad thing to tell someone.

Anyway, I'm avoiding the topic of the door b/c I don't have a good answer.

All I know is when the screen is not there. When the door is closed, the screen is there. When the door is open, the screen is there, too, unless Jean opens it for me. This is too confusing to talk about. No more *SPROINGS* for you.

I'm very happy that you love me even though I am an alpha male chauvinist poodle.

Now I'm waiting to hear about handles.

Sniffs and Licks, Lily my Love,
Your Alpha Male, Rumi Noir

Sun, May 24, 2009 10:24 PM
To: Rumi Noir
From: Lily Schott Sweetdog
Subject: Re: Dear Rumi

Dear Rumi,

You make me think. (You also make me want to sniff your butt.) I am thinking that maybe there are more bugs in West Virginia than here in Oregon because lots of times my people don't bother to close the screen. If it were always closed, I wouldn't have this problem. So you are lucky in two ways: you know for sure the screen will be closed, AND you have more bugs.

I have decided that you are not only macho but also very brave. People talk about Cancer like it's really scary, scarier than *sproings,* or mean dogs, or mean people. My person told me about how the chimp in the Portland Zoo puts out his arm and lets the vet poke him with sharp things. The chimp never says, *No, don't do that.*

I am not brave like you or that chimp. I am scared of many things, especially the handles of pots and pans. My people put dirty plates and pans on the floor for me to lick. They call me *Pre-rinse* because when I'm done, the stuff can go right back on the shelf (but they put it in the dishwasher anyhow.) So one time I was licking a delicious frying pan when suddenly it started to spin around in circles. It turned out that my he-person had kicked it by mistake. Ever since then I've become scared of pans. After six months, I went back to licking them clean, but I am still very careful. They might just start spinning.

And here's another thing I'm scared of—umbrellas. When I was a wee pup, someone pushed a button and a huge umbrella popped open in my face. I don't like them. Fortunately, here in Portland people pretend it's not raining and they don't use umbrellas.

I hope you will still respect me even though you know I am not brave.

A bunch of busy little licks to make you feel better, you big brave black Rumi.

Love, Lily

Mon, Jun 1, 2009 10:15 AM
To: Rumi Noir
From: Lily Schott Sweetdog
Subject: Concerned

Dear Rumi,

My tail got brushed today. I wish you could see it with your eyes and your nose and your tongue. It's all floaty and beautiful like a fountain. Sometimes I turn around or roll myself into a ball just to admire it. Ah, what we females suffer for beauty.

I am concerned about you. My person says instead of worrying, I should say hello and send my good wishes. At first, I didn't want to because of two reasons. One, I don't want you to think about being sick. I was hoping a squirrel or something was on your mind instead. And second, I wonder if you don't like me after I told you I'm not brave. I can bark loud and scare people, but most of the neighbors just say, *Oh, Lily,* and then I shut up and put my head where they can pat it.

I drank some green water from the slough down by the Columbia River and I didn't feel like eating for a couple of days, but then I found the backbone of something very dead and felt much better. Last night I licked all the dinner dishes—the chicken and Portobello mushroom sausage, the slender spring asparagus with lemon and grated cheese, and the tomato and pepper salad with garlic-yogurt dressing. You should have been here, Rumi. I would have shared it all with you. The people didn't give me any beer, though. It was an IPA, which is dry-hopped at the end and some people say it is bitter, but other people like it a lot. I have never had beer because you can't lick the inside of a bottle. I do like my people to have beer or wine because they smile at me more.

So what's on your furry mind today?

I'm thinking about how much I love you.

Your pen pal, Lily

Mon, Jun 1, 2009 8:41 PM
To: Lily Schott Sweetdog
From: Rumi Noir
Subject: Re: Concerned

Dear Lily,

I wish I could see and sniff your fountain of a champagne tail. Then I'd poke my nose into the center of your fluffy self when you're curled into a ball.

Do you really love me? Oh, Lily, I love you, too. I have since the beginning, Champagne-on-Snow Lady. I was scared to quivering when you chastised me for bragging about my manliness.

I haven't been thinking about squirrels, but about trucks (of course) and what I want to say to you about bravery and pan handles. Being suspicious of pans that have attacked you is not cowardly; it is intelligent. I suspect you are a sensitive, aware female dog who thinks about things that I might not notice. I wish I could be standing by your side when one of those uppity pans spins its handle at you. I'd grab that handle and the next time it wouldn't have one to spin. Just like those great clanking, smelly, growly things that roar by in the street. If I could run like I used to and get away from Jean, I know I could bring one down.

Yesterday I chased two sets of ducks down a steep bank into the water.

Jean thought I was going to swim, but even though I'm a big poodle and a rock star, swimming is against my principles. Does Mick Jagger swim? What about Bob Dylan? See what I mean?

The frustrating thing is that I caught one of those fat, self-satisfied Kanawha River ducks by the neck one time because those ducks don't believe any dog can escape from their human long enough to grab them. Well, I got that one with Jean still hanging onto my lead. I was that fast. Now Jean lets go of the lead b/c she knows I won't run up the other hill to the road when I'm done climbing the hill from the water. I wish I could surprise her. I need her a lot. I want her to touch me. I sit against her leg, preferably on her foot. I go to bed and then come back downstairs b/c I want to be near her. And it's not easy climbing up and down those shiny wooden stairs b/c the Cancer's mainly in my shoulder. I'm a little scared, to tell the truth.

So knowing that I'm loved by a beautiful female dog named Lily-Champagne-on-Snow is more wonderful than I can explain.

I'm going to lie down & think about that—and the tail you want me to see and sniff and lick.

Sniffs, licks, and—most of all—Love,

Rumi Noir

p.s. We don't have green water here, but I want you to please stay away from it. Jean is drinking too much wine. I just stare at her.

Fri, Jun 12, 2009, 11:26 am
To: Rumi Noir
From: Lily Schott Sweetdog
Subject: reminder

Dear Jean,

Please remind Rumi to write to me. I am lying here on the rug licking my underside and waiting for something to happen.

Tell him that when I ran after the garbage truck, the man threw me a biscuit. It wasn't an excellent biscuit—it was stale—but I ate it to encourage his good behavior.

Your bored friend, the Divine Ms. Lily, aka Lilypalooza

p.s. I don't want to say I am worried about him, but you can tell him there was also a FedEx truck here this morning and he would have liked it. When I barked at the driver, he laughed at me. I need consoling. The truth is, I am a very needy dog under all my beautiful fur.

Tue, Jun 23, 2009 3:18 PM
To: Rumi Noir
From: Lily Schott Sweetdog
Subject: query

Dear Jean,

Has Rumi lost his taste for correspondence? I'd appreciate a quick woof.

Love, Lily

p.s. Scratch the top of his right ear for me.

Wed, Jun 24, 2009 11:35 AM
To: Lily Schott Sweetdog
From: Jean Anaporte
Subject: Re: query

Dear Lily,

You are so dear to keep asking.

Rumi died. Wednesday morning I took him to get a shot that would stop his big heart. A week ago today. I held him and sang while the teary doctor put the needle in his left leg vein.

Rumi watched too and at the last second, he lifted his head and looked into the technician's eyes as if to ask, *What's happening?* She said he looked peaceful, but did she say that to make me happy? I don't know.

Our best moment was last Monday when I almost took him in to the doctor but his first human wanted to see him one more time. We lay on the bed. I was singing his song to him when he stretched out his good leg, put his paw on my arm, and looked into my eyes for a long time. I knew he knew he was very sick or maybe dying, and he wanted me to know that he knew I loved him, and to let me know he loved me too.

Rumi was a very difficult Alpha Male who taught me that the human variety can't be held completely responsible for their behavior. He loved me.

Here's a letter he began to you around 15 June but did not have a chance to finish. I know he would have added that he wished he could soothe your hurt feelings by lying tight against you and sniffing your beautiful tail...

Dear Lily,

Jean told me she had received an email letter from you. I think you must be the smartest female dog in the world asking for comfort and reminding me of your sensitivity and beautiful fur at the same time.

Those truck men are not sensitive (except for the garbage man who gave you a biscuit). Mostly they have the brains and attitudes of dinosaurs. That's why I bark at them, and I know that last month even I could have caught one if Jean had let me loose.

(Rumi was too sick to write more.)

Love,
Jean
And love from Rumi, who believed he was going to go see you someday and really sniff and lick you.

Thu, Jun 25, 2009 11:53 PM
To: Jean Anaporte (and Rumi Noir)
From: Lily Schott Sweetdog
Subject: Emailing: Dear Rumi last letter.doc

Dear Rumi,

You are just as real and alive for me as you have been ever been. I think I can smell you. You smell very macho. I will always remember how brave you are and will try not to be so worried about whether someone likes me or not. I will think of you chasing trucks and catching them too. Maybe I can learn from you.

Once I had the idea that someday my person would take me to West Virginia so you and I could run and snuggle, but if you're not there then I don't want to go to West Virginia anymore, wherever that silly place is. Now I am wondering if, since you are gone, West Virginia is gone too. It might as well be.

My person is crying as she is writing this down for me. I think maybe she also loved you a little, or maybe she is crying thinking about how sad your person must be. She says it's sad not to have anyone furry to cuddle with.

I forgive you for being macho. You probably couldn't help it. I know the male person in our house can't help it. Sometimes when he's having trouble with something else, he gets mad at me. Then he says he's not mad at me, but first he hurts my feelings by yelling a little. My lady person does not yell. Even when I run away on our walks and roll in exquisitely stinking messes and take a long time coming back, she doesn't yell at me. The meanest thing she does is give me a bath. I guess you will never have to bathe again.

If your person will send my person a street address, I will send a piece of my fur to your house, so that when you come back in the night to make sure Jean is okay without you, you can smell me. Also, my person has some vague idea of making something for you and me—a little illustrated book of our letters. If she ever does it, I'll remind her to send it to your person. (Of course, she doesn't always do all the things she thinks of doing. Or sometimes it takes her a long time to get around to doing them. Like years.)

Oh, Rumi. Beautiful, handsome, brave Rumi Noir. I am very sad now, but I will never be sorry that we were friends. I still love you,

Lily
I will always love you.

Sun, Jun 28, 2009 9:39 PM
To: Lily Schott Sweetdog
From: Jean Anaporte
Subject: Re: Emailing: Dear Rumi last letter.doc

Lily and Penelope,

When I took Rumi to the funeral home, his lip was pulled up a little, showing a white tooth. That tooth, and his short pom-pommed tail falling out of the blue blanket, gathered all my tenderness. Back home, I saw his house and his bed. The blankets and pad were scrambled. He had pushed them aside due to his pain. That morning had been the worst. Even an extra pain pill hadn't helped. He never cried. When I took him out to pee and poop he chose to walk down the porch steps himself and all the way to a grassy place. When he was finished, he looked around and sniffed in different directions, then looked at me without moving. I knew he wanted me to carry him back.

It so happens, Lily, that when Rumi knew he was going to die, he instructed me to cut enough ear and tail fur so I could send some to you, so please have your lady person send your address. I believe his spirit will return for a visit if I—and a little of your fur—are here. Our address is 4 Arlington Court, Charleston, West Virginia 25301.

Lily, the letter your person typed for you made me cry. It still makes me cry each time I read it. Crying is a good thing. I cried in a frightening way the day Rumi died, but not since then—until I received your letter. Your human is right—it is hard to be without a furry being to cuddle. I am glad you are there for her to snuggle with whenever she feels the loss of her mother.

You are generous in your love, Lily. Rumi knew a lot about being brave, but I think he might have learned some things about love if he'd been able to run and snuggle with you and sniff your plumey champagne-on-snow tail and let you smell how macho he was.

I send you long strokes on your silky fur.

I send your woman person a hug and much gratitude.

Don't forget to send your address.

Jean

Mon, Jun 29, 2009 10:42 PM
To: Jean Anaporte
From: Lily Schott Sweetdog
Subject: Our soul is in our fur

Dear Jean and Rumi,

For dogs, a little bit of our soul is in our fur. Maybe that's true with people too. My person has some of her father's hair in a box. Her mother's hair was mostly all gone by the time she died.

I will send you some general fur, plus ear fur, plus tail fur. I bet you can tell the difference. My person says she wants a tail just like mine. She says she would cut tail holes in her clothes if she could have such a wonderful tail.

Rumi, I will like having a little bit of your soul here in my house in Oregon at 507 NW Skyline Crest Road, Portland, Oregon 97229, Rumi. (I told Penelope to write *Rumi* twice, at both ends of that sentence, because I like saying your name. It's like you're still here.) Rumi, you will always have my heart, but I can't send it to you right now as I am using it. And if Jean has a photo that shows all your handsomeness, maybe she could send it to me and I could see you.

You have taught me so much. I will try to be brave like you. You have also shown me how much kindness and appreciation a male dog can have. When my male person gets gruff, I will remember that he is just being macho. Maybe he is remembering a time he almost caught a duck and someone took it away.

Goodnight, wherever you are. I still love you.
Lily

Wed, Jul 01, 2009 9:42 PM
To: Lily Schott Sweetdog
From: Jean Anaporte
Subject: Re: Our soul is in our fur

Dear Lily and Penelope,

When I saw the subject line, I thought one of you had sent a poem. I'd love to get a poem. I, too, have been thinking about where the soul is located. Hair and nails keep growing when we die.

I've found some pictures of Rumi (how could I select just one?) and will take them to be copied tomorrow. Then I'll tie together some ear and tail fur.

Just so you know, the package will soon be on its way to you.

Tonight, a woman walking two dogs stopped as she passed me and said, *Where is your poodle?* and then gave her condolences. I feel fortunate.

And then I remembered Rumi Noir touching my arm with his paw while I sang his song, and looking me in the eye. He was not cuddly, but we connected deeply in that moment and I could feel his intelligence. He wanted to be a free dog.

Looking forward to the fur sample from Lily. And I'd love a picture, too. Lily, I'll place it on my nightstand with your fur for when RN comes around.

Goodnight, you two.
Love and a play-bow, Jean

Letter by U.S. Mail with two small fur clippings enclosed:

July 2, 2009
Dear Jean,

Okay, here's the fur my person promised to send. Please note: my ear fur is NOT dirty. It is golden. My tail has some gold too, but that's not the part she cut. I love Rumi and I know he wouldn't have wanted me to ruin my plume.

I keep thinking of things I should have told him. We didn't have enough time. I bet he would have liked to know that my birth mom was a golden retriever and my dog father was a standard poodle *(blanc)*. I inherited his curly fur and her fancy tail.

We took some pictures today on our morning walk and will send them to you soon. Put them where Rumi will see them without having to open a drawer. When he comes back in your dreams, it will be hard for him to open drawers.

Is he really dead? How can I still love him so much? I know you do, too. Maybe he still loves us. I bet he does.

Lily

The Story is Over But This Part is IMPORTANT,
So Don't Forget to Read It!!!
It was Written by ME, Lily (mostly)!!!

Somebody told me Rumi Noir was named after a dead poet whose name was also Rumi. (No wonder you were a poet, Rumi. I don't know of any poets named Lily. Maybe I am Lily-the-First, Great Mole Killer.)

Anyhow, Jean wanted a poem, and I've been reading poems by that old guy Rumi, and I think he understood our love story. Here are four real things the long-ago Rumi wrote about us. They are all IMPORTANT, so each one will get its own page.

Here goes:

People (Rumi wrote *people*, but he meant *dogs*) **_are going_**
back and forth
across the doorsill where the two worlds meet.

That's true. I like to go back and forth over the doorsill. When my people leave the door open, I go out and in a lot. Otherwise I have to woof for them to open the door. Door handles are too high. And of course there's that little problem of the screen.

***Everything in the universe is a dog dish
brimming with wisdom and beauty.***

(He spelled it *pitcher* but he meant *dog dish*.)

Come out of the circle of time and into the circle of love.

That is what you and I did, Rumi. We also came out of the circle of distance. And now I will go on loving you beyond the circle of death. And I will always believe that you still love me.

And last, and I am trying hard to believe this,

Joy lives concealed in grief.

Dearest Rumi Noir, for the rest of my life, whenever I roll in green goop, I will miss you and I will also be sharing my joy with you.*

That's a promise. Dog's honor.

---

* especially if it's really, really smelly